Mary Didn't Know

A Country Christmas

Bree Weeks

Lone Oak Publishing, LLC

Cover by: Cover Girl Design

To Mom.

Thank you for nurturing my love for Christmas and for writing. I hope I made you proud.

(Although I'm very glad you never read my books. LOL)

I miss you.

Chapter One

MARY

The ringing phone startles me, and I smile as I check the screen. "How's the weekend with the family going?"

"Just about the way you'd think."

My best friend, Melea, had until recently been my sister-in-law. Sort of. Her husband, Jordan, is still close with his late first wife's family because of his business and their children. My ex-husband is Jordan's late wife's brother. Charles Dawson. The lying cheater. I was not aware of his philandering during our marriage, but according to everyone, I should've been. Looking back on it now, I realize how obvious it was. All the signs were there, just like you'd see in a movie or on television. But I was either too in love, too trusting, or too stupid to pick up on any of them. Maybe all three.

Lipstick on his collar that was not my shade.

The scent of perfume on his clothes that I don't wear.

Unfamiliar earrings under the seat of his car.

Just thinking about it, knowing what I now know, makes me feel like an idiot. Melea had been the one person who tried to support me, both before and after the divorce. Well, Jordan was supportive, too. He and Charles have had a difficult relationship over the years and have never gotten along. They have to work together, so it's a little awkward.

"It's going that well, is it? Glad I missed it, then."

"Well, I'm not. I've wished you were here so many times over the last couple of days, especially when I took the kids Black Friday shopping yesterday. You should've seen the kids. You'd have been so proud. They had their lists and strategies mapped out by Thursday after dinner. Then they marched through those crowded stores like little shopping veterans. I think they found almost everything they had on their lists. They won't let me help them, though. Jordan said they have some surprises for me, so I'm not allowed to see their lists or help them wrap anything."

I chuckle at her feigned frustration. "Glad y'all had fun. I know how important being with your family has been for you."

"Oh, trust me, hon. I'm always grateful to spend time with Jordan and the kids, but the rest of the extended family is for the birds. I know I don't have to convince you, though."

"No, you don't. I remember. Has great-aunt Patricia told you a million times already how she used to take all the kids shopping on Black Friday, long before it was called Black Friday, and they'd get everything done in just a few hours?"

"Three times already. Then, of course, she added that they'd come home and wrap everything that night."

"Oh, of course. How could I forget?" We laugh and then grow silent for a moment. There's another question I want to ask her, but I'm not sure how she'll take it.

Luckily, she knows me well enough that I don't have to bother. "Charles was here, in case you wanted to know."

"I didn't." I lie.

"Then I suppose you don't want to know if he brought someone or not. He did, but it's not what you think. He brought a friend of his from college. A guy. They ran into each other a couple of months ago at convention and discovered they'd both recently divorced. I think they went a little wild in Vegas, but who doesn't? Anyway, he's in town on business, and they canceled his flight, so Charles talked him into having dinner with us on Thanksgiving. His flight home left this morning, but don't ask me where his home is, because I've already forgotten. He was nice, and very cute, but I ignored both of them, mostly in protest of Charles."

Desperate to change the subject from my cheating ex-husband, I say, "Well, I'm glad you had fun with the kids, and I'm so glad you called me. But I need to run. I'm spending the afternoon with my sketchbook while I watch a little football. It *is* the Iron Bowl today, after all."

"Now you know I'm oblivious to your sports references, so I'll just ignore that last part. Don't forget to send pics of your latest creations. I love looking at them."

"Oh, before I go, I meant to tell you something else. I saw you ordered a bunch of Christmas cards from my online shop. You don't have to do that, you know. You're my best friend, not a customer. I'll send you whatever you want."

"Nonsense! I know that website you use charges for you to list things, so at least I can help you with those. It's my pleasure. Besides, I'd rather get all my handmade stuff from your shop so I can tell everyone I know where they can get them, too. People always ask me, so this way, I can send them a link to your store."

"Well, thank you for that. I'm not hurting financially, though. I got a good settlement in the divorce, and it's plenty to tide me over until my business takes off. It looks like it could be back to profitable early next year. Taking the time off really hurt my sales, but I've had a great November so far."

"You needed that time for your mental health. Don't ever be ashamed of that. Until you're profitable, I'm happy to support you. Even after then, if necessary. You know that! I love you. I miss you. Call me anytime."

She's always been such a good friend to me, and after I end the call, I miss her already. I appreciate her supporting me. It wouldn't surprise me if she spent a small fortune buying multiples of everything in my shop.

That's why I hate lying to her.

But I can't tell her my business is failing.

***

Who in the world is dumb enough to schedule a meeting first thing on Monday after a holiday? Oh, yeah. That would be me. I thought I'd be down in the dumps after spending Thanksgiving alone, and was worried that I'd need something to distract me. My thought process was flawed, and I'm now kicking myself for doing this. It's bad enough for me to deal with an accountant anyway, but to start off the week is just not working for me. Numbers are not my strong suit. I'd much rather get lost in my designs.

"So, what did you want to talk to me about, Cricket? I hope it's that you and Jack have set a date."

"We're still working on that. His family is being, let's just say, difficult."

"Again?"

"No. Still is the correct word. They've never stopped, you know."

"Sorry. Dealing with family can be a bitch."

"Yeah. Anyway, I wanted to talk about simplifying your year-end reporting, but instead I'm afraid I have some upsetting news I have to share."

Thoughts of inaccurate tax returns and other reports fill my mind. Starting my new business with financial crimes isn't the way I wanted to do this. "Was there something wrong with the business applications? I filled everything out the way I thought you instructed me. If I did something wrong, can I fix it?"

"Oh, no, Mary. It's nothing like that. I'm afraid it is serious, though. While shopping on Black Friday, my assistant noticed Christmas cards and other items that closely resemble your designs."

"What? Are you sure they're like mine?"

"Positive. She brought them in to work this morning. I'll send some images to you. Of course, I don't have your artistic eye, but they look exactly the same to me. Does anyone else have access to your designs before you produce the final products?"

"No. Well, just my assistant, but she's a dear friend of the family. I've known her since childhood. I trust her implicitly."

"Anyone who could have a motive to want to steal from you or hurt your business?"

"I can't think of anyone. What does this mean for my business? I'm sure if they're being sold in a large store, they have a much lower price point than mine, right?"

"Yes. By a lot. They're over 60% less than yours."

My stomach lurches at hearing this. "Is there a way for me to stop them from being sold?"

"There's probably some copyright issue here with intellectual property, but I don't know enough about it to advise you. Not really my area, you know, so I wouldn't have any idea about what kind of proof you need, but I have a friend who can help. A lawyer. I think you may need her."

I know she's speaking to me, but I can't seem to focus on the actual words. The pressure in my head is too loud. *All my hard work! It could be in jeopardy.* "What am I going to do? I can't lose sales right now. You know that. I wasn't sure I'd be profitable this year, but I was hoping I'd be well on my way for next year. I have only enough money left from the divorce settlement for a few more months."

"You're panicking, and you can't do that. I want you to stay calm and just let me talk with my lawyer friend. I'll have her get in touch with you. Alright? Hang in there for me, will you?"

"I'll try. Thanks for helping me through this. Is there anything I should do right now?"

"Yeah. Keep working. That will distract you from all this. It may be a couple of days before I hear anything, so don't worry. Let's reschedule for discussing year-end. I don't think you're in the right frame of mind to talk about that right now."

Sure. Right. Don't worry. That'll be no problem for me at all. That's like telling a dog not to bark,

Chapter Two

JOE

With around three weeks to go before Christmas, my office is jumping, and I absolutely love it. This was my favorite season when I was a kid, and that hasn't changed. We try to stay busy regardless of the time of year, but sometimes the season gets to be so exciting that I have a hard time keeping my employees focused. And that includes me. The one person who stays level is my assistant. But she's a hard-ass.

She's on the phone with someone when I arrive at the office, and she doesn't look pleased. I've learned over the years to sit back and let her do her thing, because she has this amazing ability to get things done, even in impossible situations. She's been that way ever since I've known her, and I'm lucky to have her. Though I sometimes wish she'd lighten up a bit.

I patiently wait for her to get off the phone. Realizing by her tone that it might take longer than I'd hoped, I turn toward my office. She hurls her stress ball at me, and it flies just barely over my head. *Yep. She's in a foul mood already.* I pick up the ball, go back to her desk, and sit quietly in the chair across from her while she finishes her call. I feel like I'm back in school waiting for the teacher to get off the phone with, well... her. When she hangs up the phone, I ask, "What's wrong, Mom?"

"*This* is what's wrong, Joe."

She passes an envelope to me, and I flip it over to see the return address. "The U.S. Copyright Office? Aren't we expecting something from them? I thought this would be good news."

She inhales so deeply that her nostrils flare. "Well, it's not. We didn't get the approval on the latest product because we haven't been able to prove we own the rights to the art."

"There's got to be some kind of mistake."

"There was. You listening to that useless friend of yours was the mistake."

"He's not useless. He's just misunderstood." I grin, but she's not in the mood for my foolishness. "Alright. What do we need to do?"

"We have a week to submit the proper paperwork, or we have to pull the product from the stores. Then we'll have to pay the fines that have accumulated since we first started selling them. Do you have any idea how much money that is?"

"I'm guessing it's more than $10." She narrows her eyes at me, and I give her my toothiest grin, hoping that will put her in a better humor. It doesn't. "Fine. How much is this going to cost us?"

"I don't know the exact amount, but it will be substantial, considering both the fines and the lost sales. We may have to lay off some employees. And Christmas bonuses are definitely out."

Shaking my head, I ask, "Are you sure? I don't want to do that to people at any time of the year, but especially not now. Not in December. We have a lot of parents and grandparents working here. How are they going to afford Christmas gifts and food?"

"That isn't our problem, son."

"Maybe it should be!" I grip the stress ball that's still in my hand before I toss it against the wall. Thankfully, it's soft and squishy, so I don't damage anything.

"Then may I suggest you track down the person who holds the rights to these and get the proper signatures so we can file this paperwork? And do it pronto! Now, leave me alone and let me get back to work."

She shoves the papers into my hands and returns to her computer screen.

Realizing she'd dismissed me, I take the envelope to my office. I have no idea how to resolve this, but I know who can. It only takes a second for me to find the number on my phone, and it rings only once before the line goes dead. Strange. I don't normally drop calls from here. I dial it again, and the same thing happens. After the third time, I know it's not just a dropped call. He's screening my call.

Why wouldn't he want to talk to me?

I can't quite put my finger on it, but something doesn't feel right about this.

***

I try on and off for a couple of hours to call again. Every call either goes straight to voicemail or ends abruptly. Tired of going through this, I leave a message, asking for a return call about getting the proper documentation for the copyright office. The whole thing leaves me so frustrated that I decide to take an early lunch.

Mom gives me a disapproving look when I attempt to sneak past her desk, but I ignore it and keep going. It's not like that's the first time she's looked at me that way, and I'm certain it won't be the last. I make a mental note to stop by the bakery on my way back to the office to pick up some of those cupcakes she likes.

In a rare foul mood, I opt to eat in my car instead of hanging out inside the diner to chat with the crowd. Peggy gives me a wary look as she hands me my takeout order. She's known Mom since they were kids, so she normally asks about her. Not this time. Though I try not to listen, Peggy theorizes to her husband that Mom must be on my ass about something.

She's not wrong.

After lunch, I check my list to see if there's anything I need to pick up while I'm out. I hate to make special trips to the store for one or two things, so I try to combine things like that as much as I can. Though not Mom's favorite cupcakes, the ones they have in the deli are tasty. Pretty damn efficient of me to do that *and* pick up groceries.

While I'm here waiting on the cupcakes, I think of a few more things I need, so I grab a cart. Just as I'm about to head back to the deli, I remember one more thing I need to do. Mom and I talked about reports from customers about potential quality control issues with certain products last week. I want to check to see if there's any truth to that rumor. I'll also make note of how many are on the shelf and compare that against the number we sent to this store. See if they're selling as well as I hoped.

I spot her as soon as I turn the corner into the greeting card aisle.

The most beautiful woman I've ever seen in my life stands in front of me. Until this moment, I always thought that honor went to my ex-wife, but Elizabeth is a pauper next to this princess.

I quickly check my cart to make sure there's nothing embarrassing in it. An incident from when I was a teenager still haunts me to this day. Mom sent me to the store to buy Dad's incontinence products, and I ran into the prettiest girl in school. Elizabeth. She liked to joke later that we fell in love thanks to a package of adult diapers. I never found it as funny as she did.

My cart has nothing in it I wouldn't want anyone to see, just some cans of soup, a loaf of bread, and a box of crackers. So, I take a deep breath, brush my hand over my hair, and walk toward her.

I'm immediately drawn to her curves, and oh my God, she smells good! I can feel myself getting hard just standing here looking at her. She doesn't see me at first, but she must sense me staring at her. She steps away from me, not far, but enough for me to know I need to dial in the creepiness factor.

I look at the store display that seems to have as much of her attention as I have. *Shit!* She's looking at one of my company's greeting cards. I hadn't realized Mom approved the large font size of "Joe McCoy Enterprises" that's printed on the back of the cards. It looks rather garish now that I see it up close in the store lighting.

I glance quickly at this beautiful angel's face as I reach past her to take a card, too, thinking maybe that will help ease the creepiness. She'll think I'm just another shopper buying Christmas cards.

When I turn back, she's looking at me, too. I smile. "Hi, I say. These are nice cards, but I never know which one is appropriate to pick up for the occasion."

"You think these are nice cards?"

It sounds like she doesn't like them, and I wonder if I said something wrong. The business owner side of me temporarily upstaged the horny guy inside me inside me. I need to find out what she, as a customer, thinks of my product. "Well, I mean, I know precious little about greeting cards, but they seem nice to me."

"Well, they're not. They're awful. See how the ink bleeds through the paper here? And it's uneven in this spot here on the front? Those are dead giveaways that they're not of good quality. They're definitely not hand-drawn on handmade paper like the back says. I see this is a local company, and I have a good mind to call this Joe McCoy and let him know they're selling mass produced copies of someone's work. He probably knows that already, though. It's just business for him, I'm sure. He doesn't give a damn about the artist. None of these big companies do. Greedy bastards."

This isn't going the way I'd hoped just a few minutes ago when I turned the corner and saw her. Instead of getting her number, I feel the need to defend myself, and my company, against her raging.

Instead, I opt to not say a word. I truly want to know what she thinks. If there are things I need to improve with my business, it would be irresponsible to ignore a customer. Even if I find myself dreaming of filthy things to do to this fucking hot customer.

I pull myself out of thoughts of having my face between her legs and try to focus on what she's saying. Problem is, I keep staring at her lips. They make me long to feel them gently caressing my cock, leaving that pretty pink lipstick all up and down my shaft. Like she's marking her territory.

"I'm sorry to unload on you like this, especially here in the store. You've probably come here for just a few things and didn't expect to run into some crazy lady who's upset about these." She motions toward the cards display.

"No problem. I can certainly understand being upset about a product and wanting to have the company get it right. What I don't understand is why you're taking it so personally."

She frowns, and blushes slightly, which sends my temperature through the roof. If I thought I was hot for her before, it doesn't compare to anything that I'm feeling right now.

I imagine having her naked in bed beside me and what I'm doing to her is the reason she's blushing. I feel my cock stirring, and I realize if I don't stop thinking of her this way, I'll have a boner so big I won't be able to walk out of the store.

"Never mind. That was rather presumptuous of me. Forgive me. You have every right to feel exactly the way you feel without having to give explanations."

Opening and closing her mouth, I think she's about to say something. Instead, she smiles a shy smile and averts her eyes from mine. "I'd better get going. If I had any friends waiting for me, I'm sure they'd be worried by now. Nice talking with you."

As she turns to go, it hits me she may walk out of my life forever. I can't allow that to happen. "Hey, I don't even know your name."

She smiles and waves as she jogs toward the door. Because I have items in my cart and don't want to be accused of stealing them, I take a minute to figure out a place to leave it so I can run after her. By the time my head catches up with my heart, she's gone, and I've missed my chance.

Chapter Three

JOE

Mom insists on having dinner together as a family whenever we're both in town. It's a little weird, since it's just the two of us alone most of the time, unless you count the staff. She never counts them, but I always try.

"How many times do I have to ask you to not fiddle with that cell phone at the table, Joseph?"

I can tell she's pissed since she calls me Joseph. "Sorry, Mother. I'm still having trouble reaching Charles, and I'd hoped he would've called me back by now. I don't want to miss it when he does."

"Having it in your pocket to answer if he calls is one thing, but you're glancing at it every few minutes as if you expect him to call because you desire it to happen. He will not."

"Yes, I know you think that." *You've told me enough times.* "I don't think you're giving him enough credit. I've never known him to ghost me before."

"First, I assume ghost means to ignore. If so, please use the proper terms. I didn't send you to Harvard Business School to hear you use slang with me as if I'm supposed to know what you mean. Second, until recently, you haven't seen Charles, or had much contact with him at all since you were in college. You barely know the man at this point in your life. You shouldn't expect him to behave a certain way. There's been a lifetime since then and now. For both of you. Running into each other at a conference in Las Vegas, and getting into trouble while you were there, doesn't mean you're the best of friends again."

"Please don't mention the trouble in Vegas. It's embarrassing."

"Thank God it is! I didn't raise you to be a man who would be proud of his arrest for soliciting prostitutes."

"Of course, I'm not proud. And we didn't know they were prostitutes."

"I'm not sure that's the win you think it is. All that means is that you propositioned two strange women for sex. That's shameful as well."

"Could you please get back to insulting Charles? I think I liked that much better."

"Didn't you tell me he is a divorcée, the same as you?"

"No one says divorcée anymore, Mother."

"I do, so obviously some people still say it. Besides, you're missing my point."

"Why don't you get to it, then?" I say, with more irritation in my voice than I intend.

"My point, dear son, hasn't changed. I'm trying to explain to you that perhaps Charles is not the same person you knew back then. People change. Relationships change. When relationships fall apart, people sometimes suffer traumas, and I think perhaps that may be what is happening with you. Possibly Charles, too. Although it's also entirely possible that he's just a disreputable human being."

"Why? Because he's divorced? Do you think I'm disreputable, too?"

"Of course not, darling. What I'm saying is that when a relationship ends, it leaves scars. People either become stronger for the experience or they become harder for it. Maybe he's just damaged."

"Why do I get the feeling you're talking more about the demise of my relationship with Elizabeth than about my friendship with Charles?"

"Well, darling, you *did* have an affair."

"And that's the greatest regret of my life. We grew apart at least a couple of years before our divorce, and one of us should have left then. She didn't deserve the way I treated her." Mom looks satisfied, and I realize that's the con-clusion she wanted me to reach. "When did you become a psychiatrist? And I thought you didn't approve of our marriage." I ask, before I can stop myself.

"Don't be smart with me, son. I neither have the time nor the patience for the disrespect. You know what I mean, and you know that I'm right. Deep down, you know it."

I hate it when she's right. Especially when she's talking about my personal life. It's bad enough when she upstages me in business at my company, but when she treats me like a child, it's even worse. "Oh, darling. Don't be so sad. It's mother's intuition at its best. Let's change the subject, shall we? Tell me about this beautiful blonde woman you met today when you were supposed to be buying cupcakes for me."

"How the hell do you know about that?"

She smiles devilishly. "There are some advantages to liv-ing in a small town, dear. One of them is I always know what you're doing, and with whom you're doing it. A lovely young woman stealing all the hearts in the town is definitely newsworthy. Especially if one of those hearts belongs to my only son. So, tell me about her."

I can't help smiling as I think of her. "There's not much to tell. We spoke for a few minutes, and that's it."

"Is that so? Then the report I received about you being completely smitten with her is false?"

"We really going to talk about your snooping skills. They are world class. Perhaps we should open a new division at work and assist police investigations or private detectives."

"Perhaps you should stop being so snarky and tell me about this girl."

"Where did you learn the word 'snarky'?"

"Don't mind about that. I have my sources. I'm not going to ask you again about this girl."

"Promise?" She lowers her eyes to me with a look she used to give me when I was five years old. That's exactly how I feel at the moment. "Fine. She's beautiful, Mom. So sweet and kind."

The little space between Mom's eyes creases like it does when she thinks I'm full of shit. "That's not the impression I would've thought she'd left with you. I understand she was rather upset about something. Perhaps even something to do with our company?"

"Alright... do you have cameras set up all over this town? How could you possibly know that?"

"I told you, darling. I have people who tell me everything. And, when someone is degrading our company, I hear soon enough. So, do you want to tell me what made her angry?"

"Now that you mention it, I'm not really sure what happened. Or why it happened, is really more accurate. When I arrived, she was looking over the Christmas cards we just released. She was scrutinizing them, and she was complaining of their poor quality."

"Are they of poor quality?"

"Ordinarily, I wouldn't know. You know I don't pay attention to that sort of thing. But she pointed out inconsistencies in the ink and the paper that she claimed were examples of lower-end items. She thought it was criminal to call them 'handmade.' I don't know. Maybe she was right. I was really more interested in her than I was in the cards."

Just as Mother starts to ask another question, my ringing phone interrupts her. I hold up one finger toward her as I answer. "Charles! Buddy. I'm so glad you called. I've been trying to get hold of you."

Mother puts her hand behind her ear, signaling she wants me to put the call on speaker. I shake my head, but she angrily nods hers. I know when to cut my losses. Placing the phone on the table, I hit the speaker button and hear Charles's crisp baritone voice. "Sorry, buddy. I've been a little indisposed. What can I do for you?"

"Well, as I mentioned in my message, we've had some trouble getting the copyright filed for those last images you sent to me from your local artist. We finally got the prior ones approved, but they took forever. If I don't get this latest batch approved soon, I'll either have to pull the product or pay a huge fine." Mother shakes her head and mouths something to me. "Sorry... actually, I'll have to pull them *and* pay a huge fine."

"Hate to hear that, but I really need to go. Someone just stuck his head in my office."

"Wait! Charles! I just need a quick second."

I hear him sigh loudly through the phone and then distinct resignation in his voice. "Fine. What?"

"I need you to send the licenses from the artist to me. I have to prove I have legal rights to the images."

"Yeah, sure. I'll have my secretary send them. I really need to go."

Mom gives me another look that makes me feel like a child. This time, though, I don't think it's unwarranted. Something is wrong, but I can't put my finger on it.

Chapter Four

MARY

I take a deep breath and try to maintain my composure as my assistant, Paulina, tosses the cards down on my desk. "I know you said you didn't want to support the company that may have stolen your designs, but I thought it would be a good idea to see what we're up against."

"I already saw them at the store, and I don't need to see them again."

"Oh, I think you do, Mary. You actually have to do more than just look at them. You're going to have to study them. Inspect them. Make notes on how they're identical to yours. That's the only way you'll be able to prove they're stolen designs. You have the original work in your files, copyrighted and legitimized. Whoever stole these from you doesn't. You'll need to show proof."

"I know your boyfriend is a lawyer, but I can't afford to fight this. My accountant already recommended a lawyer, but I barely have enough money to keep the business running. It's just too expensive. I'm not paying myself a salary, and if I'm not careful, I won't be able to afford your wages much longer. We're just going to have to let this go and focus on something else. More designs. New ones. Have new cards made with them and forget about the older ones."

She looks at me as if she thinks I've lost my mind. And maybe I have. "You can't give up that easily. Besides, my boyfriend does everything I want, or he gets no pussy! I'll just blow him a couple of times and he'll take your case all the way to the Supreme Court."

Heat rises from my neck all the way to my face. She grins at my embarrassment as I drop my head to avoid her eyes. Returning my attention to the cards on my desk, I say, "I don't have a case, and I wouldn't want you to prostitute yourself on my behalf even if I did."

"Mary, how long has it been since you got laid?"

I gasp at her boldness, which makes her grin even wider. "I don't think that's an appropriate question for the office."

"That long, huh? You used to be married. You know men are sometimes more agreeable to do certain things if their cock is happy. Don't tell me you never used sex to gain an advantage in some situation. I won't believe it if you do. I've known you since before either of us knew what sex was. So, don't try to blow smoke up my skirts."

"Sex is a special thing, to be enjoyed in a loving relationship. It's not to be used as a bargaining chip."

"Alright, so maybe you didn't actually fuck someone to get what you wanted, but I'm sure you've flirted to get your way. Sometimes stroking a man's ego is just as effective as stroking his dick. Besides, I think some men expect a little nookie in return for something. It's not a big deal. Or maybe it is, depending on how well he's hung. My guy is extremely well-hung, and it will be my pleasure to bargain on your behalf. Trust me."

"That's enough, Paulina. I don't want to hear any more about you trading your body for legal help for me. So, please, just stop talking about it. What I really want to know is what you think about the cards from that other company and how they compare to mine."

"Oh, honey, they don't compare at all. It's obvious they're mass-produced. The runny ink, the frayed paper at the edges, and the crooked text are all pretty obvious, even to a lay person like me."

"What? I didn't see crooked text! Which one?"

She thumbs through the cards, mumbling about design inconsistencies. "Yeah, it's horrible." She passes one to me and she's absolutely right. I hadn't noticed that in the store.

"Thank you for getting these."

"So, you're not mad at me?"

"Well, I was at first, but it does make sense for me to have physical examples instead of just relying on my memory. I can make different designs and move ahead with those."

"Crap, Mary… did you see the time? Don't you have an appointment with the banker this morning?"

"Oh, God! I completely lost track of time. If I leave right now, I might make it on time. While I get my coat, will you pick out a few of your favorites of the new things in my sketchbook? I want to show Mr. Jepson at the bank what I've been working on. Hopefully that will be enough to show him what I have planned for the immediate future of the business and will increase my chances of getting the loan."

As soon as the words come out of my mouth, I realize I've made a mistake. Before I get a chance to stop her, she grabs my sketchbook and thumbs through it to the middle, showing my most recent drawings. There's one drawing I don't really want to explain, but I can see by the look in her eyes, I'm not going to have a choice.

"Who is this? He's not your ex-husband, is he? I know I only met him at your wedding, but I don't remember him looking like this."

I snatch the book from her hands, trying to think of an excuse. "No. It's not. I wouldn't draw him, anyway. He's a vile creature who spent most of our marriage in the company of other women. Some of them were friends of mine."

"Well, then who is he? He's hot!"

"You think he's hot?"

"Let me see him again."

Reluctantly, I open the book to his image and wait for my face to turn blood red as she smiles at me. "Yep. Hot enough to melt the snow they're predicting for tomorrow. Do tell. Who is he and have you fucked him yet?"

"He's just a guy I saw yesterday at the store. He was looking at the cards while I was there. I sort of talked him out of buying some of them."

"So, did you two go to dinner afterwards?"

"No. I only talked to him in the store for about five minutes. Why would you think we went to dinner?"

"He must have made quite the impression on you if you spent five minutes with the guy and you drew him in this much detail from memory."

My face flushes again as I realize she's right. He did make an impression on me. I couldn't sleep much last night because I kept seeing his face when I closed my eyes, but I couldn't tell her that. She'd never let me live it down. I wondered who he was and if I'd run into him again.

"So, what's his name?"

"I, um, I don't know. I didn't catch his name."

"Girl, you'd better find this guy and take him to bed as fast as you can. Get his name first, though."

"Why do you have to make everything sexual?"

"First, it's fun. Second, I don't make everything sexual. This I am, but not everything." I roll my eyes and she shoves the sketchbook back in my hand. "Don't look at me like that. Besides, you're late. You need to leave now. We'll talk about this later."

She's right. I don't have time to argue with her about the sketch. Or the guy. "Wish me luck," I say as I head to the door.

"Always. Let me know if you need anything from me."

***

I check my watch as I get out of the car at the bank. Only five minutes late. But still late. Never a good sign. How can I expect him to perceive me as a serious businesswoman if I don't value his time? I'll just have to see if I can make a better impression on him with my sales and reports.

No need to regret anything now. I pick up my head, push back my shoulders, and stride confidently into the bank. Whether anyone believes I am an accomplished person is yet to be seen, but I'll do my best to make sure I don't screw things up more than they already are.

The tellers are all busy with customers, so no one is looking directly at me as I go in. Good. That gives me a moment to take a deep breath and calm my nerves. Part of me wishes there was a mirror hanging in the bank's lobby, but another part is grateful there isn't. I know I must look a mess.

I look toward the back, to the offices used by the loan officers and managers. Though there's no one in any of the rooms, I'm confident that's where Mr. Jepson told me to meet him.

Standing awkwardly at the front, I finally attract a woman's attention. She's a little older than I am, but she must be the most stunning woman I've ever seen in my life. She's not classically beautiful, but I can't seem to take my eyes off her. "Hello," she says as she approaches me. "Can I help you with something?"

"Yes, hello. I have an appointment with Mr. Jepson. I'm a few minutes late, and I hope he hasn't given up on me. Is he in another part of the bank? I don't see him in his office."

"I'm so sorry. Mr. Jepson is actually at home sick today. Are you Ms. Bright?"

I nod, though my stomach does flips, disappointed I won't have the meeting with him. "Yes, I'm Mary Bright. I suppose I can call him tomorrow to see about rescheduling."

She smiles warmly. Her friendly demeanor shines through her professionalism. "That won't be necessary. Mr. Jepson asked me to cover his appointments today. I'm Grace Herndon, Executive Vice President of the branch.

If you'd come with me to my office, I have your file already open on my computer." She turns to the young woman sitting at the desk just outside her office. I hadn't noticed her before. "Elaine? Would you mind bringing some coffee to my office? Ms. Bright, would you like coffee, tea, or perhaps some water?"

"Coffee would be great. Thank you." Elaine smiles and rushes off down the hallway as Ms. Herndon motions for me to go into her office and have a seat.

I take a deep breath as I sit and attempt to make myself comfortable. Before my divorce, I had no problems in social situations. Melea used to joke that I could carry on conversations with princes and paupers. And she was right. I could, and I did.

Charles had business connections all over the world, and he loved taking me with him as arm candy. He used the old JFK line about being the man who accompanied me to whichever city we were in. It flattered me at first, but then I realized how degrading it was. Not when JFK said it about Jackie, because that was brilliant. But when Charles said it about me, it didn't feel like a compliment. It felt like a complaint.

My self-esteem took a hit when my marriage fell apart. With all my security gone, both financial and emotional, it took a while for me to have the confidence I needed to make good decisions. Being in the presence of such a striking, professional, and completely put together woman makes all those feelings come back.

We discuss the weather and the busy nature of the holiday season as we wait for Elaine to bring our coffee. Once that's on the desk in front of us, Ms. Herndon shifts her focus to business. "So, Ms. Bright, you own a small art business?"

"Yes. And please call me Mary. I'm still getting used to the name Bright. I recently divorced, and I wanted to reinvent myself completely. So, when the judge said I could choose a new last name if I wanted, I chose Bright. I knew I wanted to start this business, and I thought it would be a good name for my brand. Greeting cards have been my first product line, and it amused me to think of a woman named Mary Bright designing Christmas cards. I'm still getting all the legal documents, but I'm hoping it's all done by the end of the year."

"What a charming story! Is that in your company's bio somewhere?" she asks while flipping through some of the brochures I'd also previously sent to Mr. Jepson. When I shake my head, she says, "Well, it should be. I think you're right. As a woman, I'd love to support a business like yours. You should let customers know exactly who you are. Tell them your story. Give them a way to connect with you."

I smile nervously. "You sound like my assistant. She tells me the same thing." I regret my words the moment I say them. *Did I really just compare this professional and accomplished Executive Vice President of the bank to my immature and sex-crazed assistant?* What impact will that have on her decision to give me the loan?

If she's insulted, I can't tell. She smiles just as warmly as before. "Well, she sounds like a very intelligent woman." She takes a delicate sip of her coffee and returns her attention to the computer screen. "Let's see what we have here. I've already reviewed the financials you sent to Mr. Jepson, and everything seems in order. Your credit score is excellent."

"Does that mean you're approving the loan?" I ask, hopefully.

She looks directly into my eyes and says, "Mary, your credit score, bank statements, and cash flow reports aren't the only things we review in making that kind of determination. We also look at your business history and projections for at least a few quarters. I'm afraid you have little information that supplies us with those numbers. Tell me, how long have you been in business again?"

"Not long. Just this year. But I've had good sales, sort of." *Well, this certainly isn't coming out the way I imagined.* "Look, I know I haven't been in business long enough to be able to show you good financial statements, but I work really hard, and I pour my heart into my designs. I really need this loan to push my company forward."

She inhales and looks at me sympathetically. *Yep. She's turning me down.* "I'm sorry, Mary. Truly. I wish I could help you. If it were up to me, I'd approve the loan right now. But we have guidelines, and I must adhere to them, no matter how much I disagree with them. My advice to you is to keep working to improve your sales and decrease your expenses. As much as I hate to think of someone losing a job, you might reconsider having an assistant, or perhaps cut down on her hours."

Though most of her records are on the computer, I glance at her desk and see a balance sheet I'd sent to Mr. Jepson with handwritten notes on it. I squint to read the words on the page, and fury fills me when I make out what's written there. I point to the notes before she closes the file. "What is this?"

She looks down and sees the note, and her head snaps up. "I didn't write that, Mary."

"Who did?" I demand. "Who wrote that it would be a good idea for me to ask my ex-husband for the loan instead of the bank?"

She stammers for a moment, which shocks me, considering how professional and kind she's been since I arrived. "I'm not sure, but I'm appalled to see it. That's certainly not the way I feel about it."

I want to believe her, but rage fills my entire body, and before I can stop myself, I stand and look at her accusingly. "Do you even know my ex-husband, Ms. Herndon?"

"No, I don't."

"Well, if you knew anything at all about him, you'd know what kind of man-whore he is. I have no intention of ever speaking to him again, much less asking him for money. I'd rather starve or be homeless. Or both. To imagine that anyone would write such a thing on my paperwork is unthinkable!" I gather my things, including the paperwork on her desk, and loudly head for the door. "I'll be closing my account here as soon as possible! I refuse to support a place such as this!"

The other customers in the bank, as well as the employees, have noticed me. How could they not? I take advantage of the attention. "And I suggest that all of you do the same thing. Why on earth anyone would want to do business with a bank that insults you is beyond me."

As I begin to storm out of the building, one person catches my eye. How could I miss him? The guy from the store yesterday who was talking with me about the cards. The one I drew in my sketchbook. *Oh God! I think I might be sick. He saw me making an ass of myself.* Well, I can't do anything about that now, so I just keep walking.

His arm reaches for me as I pass by him, and I reluctantly allow him to stop me. "Hey. I know you probably don't remember me, but we met yesterday. Are you alright? What's wrong?"

I want to tell him, but I know if I stop now, I won't be able to control my emotions, and I really don't want him to see me cry. I shake my head, lower my eyes to the floor, and keep moving.

Chapter Five

JOE

The beautiful woman I haven't been able to get out of my mind has just gotten out of my grasp. And again, I didn't get her name.

When I saw her going into the bank as I was getting breakfast across the street, I thought I was fortunate and that I'd be able to find out all I wanted to know about her. I had to think of a good excuse to be at the bank, so she won't think I'm stalking her.

But with the scene she just caused, my being here is likely the least of her worries.

Once the customers settle down, I notice movement in the back-office area and move in that direction. "You can't go back there, Joe. Not right now."

"Look, Arthur. I know you're the security guard and your job is to keep people under control, but you know I have to talk to her. You're welcome to shoot me if you want to stop me."

"Naw, man. You know I won't do that. I just need to make it look like I'm trying to stop you… put on a good show for the boss when he watches the footage from the security cameras. Just don't cause any trouble, will ya?"

I nod and grin as he sits back down in the chair near the tellers, and I continue to the offices in the back. She doesn't see me step inside, but it appears that she's too rattled to jump when she suddenly hears my voice. "Gracie? What just happened? Are you alright?"

"Joe? What are you doing here?"

I can't tell her that I was here to get close to that gorgeous creature who just yelled at her and stormed out of her office. Luckily, Elaine comes in before I can answer her.

"Grace? What the hell?"

"I'm fine, Elaine. Don't worry. Just get back to work, please. Let's try to return to normal as quickly as possible." She sits and puts her head in her hands.

"You can go ahead and get the bottle of Scotch out of your desk. I won't tell anyone."

This time, she does jump at the sound of my voice but motions for me to shut the door and pull the blinds. "Grab a couple of glasses out of the cabinet, will you? Surely you'll want one, too."

Though it's still a little early in the day, I figure it's 5:00 somewhere, so why not? I place the glasses on her desk and watch as the amber liquid splashes in them. I notice that her glass is distinctly fuller than mine, but I say nothing. She's had a hell of a morning. "So, are you going to tell me what happened, Gracie?"

"Do you know you're the only person in the world, other than Grandma, who calls me Gracie?"

"And I'm not going to stop, either. If it's good enough for that woman, it's good enough for me."

She chuckles and takes a sip of her drink as the glow of the alcohol spreads across her face. "You know, she always wanted me to marry you. She was furious with me when I let you slip out of my hands."

"If she'd only known what you did with your hands, it would've been a shotgun wedding, or she would've sent you to a convent."

"She *did* know, Joe. She's the one who found me in the bathroom when I miscarried our baby and insisted I go to the hospital. If it weren't for her, I might have bled to death." She smiles at me through the tears she's desperately trying to hold back. "I'm sorry I didn't tell you about the baby until it was too late. I was young, stupid, and terrified. But you had a right to know the truth. I just didn't want you to feel obligated. I'm not really sure why I'm telling you this now. Seeing people upset brings out these emotions in me, I suppose."

I stretch out my hand to take hers and squeeze. Somehow, it's soft yet firm at the same time. Just like her. Like most women I know. "Water under the bridge, honey. Water under the bridge. I'm sorry I wasn't there for you when you needed me."

"You were off at college, and I didn't expect you to drop everything to come back to this little town to take care of me. Your mother would've shot me, anyway."

"She'd have shot us both." As she finishes her drink, I pick up the bottle, questioning if she'd like a refill. She shakes her head and says, "Better not. It wouldn't look good to get drunk at work, especially with the disaster this day's been so far. I'm glad you're here to talk with me, Joe."

"Well, you looked a little stressed, and I figured you'd need a friend. Now, what happened?"

She throws her head back in her chair and makes a disgusted sound. "Oh, it was so stupid, and I have a good mind to fire Len Jepson for doing something like this. So, I suppose you heard that woman yell at me as she left my office a few minutes ago, right?" I nod. "Do you know her, by the way? I saw you try to speak with her as she left."

"We've met, sort of. I briefly spoke with her, but I don't know who she is or even her name."

"Her name is Mary, and well, she's a sweet girl. Smart, too. And talented. Anyway, she came in to discuss a business loan, but she doesn't qualify, and no matter my personal feelings in wanting to support women-owned small businesses, my hands are tied. I could get fired if I approved it. I tried to give her some suggestions, but she seemed a little desperate and didn't want to wait to follow them and apply again in the future."

"So, she got mad because you wouldn't give her the loan?"

"No. It's worse than that. Before she came in, I was looking over the paperwork that Jepson had, because her appointment was actually with him. He's out sick today, so I met with her instead. Anyway, that jackass had written on the bottom of the balance sheet that she should ask her rich ex-husband for the money instead of wasting his time. I saw the note and tried to hide it from her, but I wasn't fast enough. She saw it and was highly offended. And I don't blame her. It offended me *for* her! I tried to play stupid and act like I hadn't seen it, but I don't think she believed me. And by then, she wouldn't let me explain. She was hurt and angry and stormed out of here. She seemed like such a sweetheart. I'll bet she didn't even make it to her car before she started to cry."

I take a deep breath, grateful to know why my beautiful angel was upset, but also upset at the idea of her having an ex-husband. "You're right. She didn't. Actually, she didn't make it out the front door before she was crying. I could see the tears as she walked past me. What's this about her ex-husband? He's wealthy?"

"I don't know. He is, according to Jepson's note, at least, though I have no idea who the man is. She said something about him cheating on her a lot, so I suppose he was an ass to her. In my way of thinking, it's a good thing she got away when she did."

Trying not to appear desperate to find out all I can about the woman of my dreams, I hesitate to ask more questions. Besides, if I know Gracie, she likely already thinks I'm interested. Why else would I be asking so many questions? "That's a shame. No woman should have to deal with a cheating spouse."

"Sorry, Joe. Present company excluded, of course."

"No. You're right. I was an ass for cheating on Elizabeth, and I'll always have to live with that. Maybe it's a good thing it happened... or at least it's a good thing we're not together any longer. I understand that she's happier than she's ever been in her life."

"She is."

From the flush in her face, it's obvious she's still in contact with my ex-wife, and she's not ready to tell me about that. I decide not to call her on it. She likely didn't mean to let that slip. I can bring that up with her some other time. Maybe when she's not so upset.

Despite my better judgment, I press my luck by asking more questions. "So, who is this guy? This rich guy who cheated on that sweet and smart woman who just stormed out of your office?"

Elaine sticks her head in the door before Grace can answer me. "Sorry to interrupt you guys. Grace, you'd better pick up line 2. It's the boss."

"Great! I guess he's already heard about what happened here this morning. I wonder which one of those busybodies called him. Doesn't matter, though. I knew he'd find out, eventually. Another couple of hours and the whole town will know about it. Sorry to cut this short, Joe. I guess it's time to take my medicine."

"No problem." I lie. It's absolutely a problem for me, but I have to respect her. She's already picking up the phone and waving at me reluctantly as I start to leave. I nod in acknowledgment and close the door behind me.

"Don't worry, Joe," Elaine says, as I hesitate in front of her desk. "I'll make sure to wash those glasses and return the bottle to its hiding place before anyone here can gossip about it. Lord knows they'll be plenty to talk about without spreading a rumor about Grace getting drunk at work. Who knows? They may even blame you."

"Not surprising in the least. Wouldn't be the first time, and I'm sure it wouldn't be the last. What would we all do without you taking care of us, Elaine?"

"Let's hope you never have to find out. And yes, she still keeps a box of breath mints in her purse." She winks and smiles as she answers her own ringing phone.

I wave to her and leave the building. Despite the other people here attempting to wave to me also, I have no interest in greeting any of these gossiping fools. I ignore them all and focus on how to find out more about my beautiful mystery woman.

Chapter Six

MARY

I don't that the wherewithal to leave the parking lot of this wretched place. The humiliation is simply too great. I can't believe anyone would be so cruel as to suggest something so rude and crass, especially in a business situation. Though I never met that horrible Mr. Jepson, I spoke with him over the phone, and we exchanged emails. He seemed so nice. Boy, was I wrong!

And Ms. Herndon... well, she just seemed so professional. *When will I ever learn to become a better judge of character?*

I pick up the phone to call the one person I know who will always support me. But the call goes to voicemail, and, as badly as I hate it, I have no choice but to leave a message. "Hey, Melea. It's me. Sorry to bother you when I know you're getting ready for the Christmas concert with the kids tonight, but I just wanted to say hello. Well, that and to cry, at least virtually, on your shoulder. It's been a tough day, and it's not even lunchtime. I really need a friendly voice right now. Call me back when you get this message. Love you!"

"Hey... are you alright?"

I jump as I hang up the phone and turn to see my dream guy knocking at my car window. I take a deep breath and glance in the mirror to see how red my eyes are before rolling down the window. I look horrible, but there's not much I can do about it now. "Hi again. Yes, I'm fine, thank you. I didn't mean to cause a scene in there. I should probably go now."

Before I can start the ignition, he leans down and looks at me, studying me carefully. His eyes are the color of the sky. My heart skips a beat, and the space between my legs tingles. I try to regain my composure before I pull him into the car with me and enjoy his body right here in the bank parking lot in front of God and everybody.

"I'm Jo— Joshua, by the way. I figured with as many times we're run into each other, I should probably introduce myself." He sticks his hand through the open window, and I shake it. I notice he hesitated when he said his name. Strange. *Does he not want to tell me who he is? I suppose anyone who witnessed my blowup in the bank would be a little wary of me.*

"Mary," I say. "Look, like I said, I'm sorry for causing a scene back there, but I need to go. I need to get back to work."

"Sure. Yeah, I understand. So do I. But I saw you out here, and I knew it had been a few minutes since you left the bank. Plenty of time for you to have left. So, I was just making sure you were alright. You know. Not too upset that you couldn't drive."

"That's very nice of you, Joshua, but it's not necessary. I'm fine. Thank you, but if you'll excuse me. I don't want to hurt your arm when I drive off." *Why am I in such a hurry to get away?* I've thought about nothing except him since the time I saw him yesterday, and now I'm pushing him away? Am I simply a glutton for punishment?

"Mary," he says with an intensity to his voice that sends shivers up and down my spine, and directly into my core. "I'd like to take you to dinner tonight, if you're free."

I have to fight to keep my heart from beating out of my chest. *Did he just ask me out?* My head is telling me one thing, but my body is telling me something else. Something completely opposite. He leans forward, putting his lips dangerously close to mine. The fight inside me just went in the next round. Now my pussy is getting involved in the struggle.

He glances at my chest, and I realize my nipples are pushing through my bra, begging for him to take them into his mouth and suck until I can't take the pleasure any longer. I've never had this kind of visceral reaction to a man before, not even when I met Charles. And I've certainly never experienced this with someone I've known for a combined total of ten minutes.

Despite the alarm bells going off in my head about slowing things down, my body wins the battle. Something inside tells me there's something special happening here, though I can't quite put my finger on it. As I look deeper into his eyes, I think how easily I could fall into them. And when I realize he's looking at me the same way, it's almost too much for me to bear. I think I realize now what Paulina means when she talks about instalove. Or instalust, more likely. Dirty and delicious thoughts enter my mind, but I resist the urge to tell him how badly I want to fuck him right here and right now. I can't even imagine where those thoughts are coming from, but my desire is undeniable.

He's still watching my chest heave up and down, and I'm enjoying the look that crosses his face. Hunger. That's what he's manufacturing in me. Hunger. For him. For us. For pleasure. Forever.

I lick my lips, and despite the dryness in my mouth, I manage to say, "I'd like that."

He smiles through the hungry expression on his face, similar to mine. The heat between us is electrifying. My head spins and his face is all I see.

"Great," he says. He pulls himself away from me and stands up. "May I see your phone? I'll put the details in your calendar."

I mindlessly hand him my phone and watch his fingers dance across the screen. I imagine what those same fingers might do to my pussy, and I have to clamp my legs together to suppress the feeling. My eyes roam over his fit body as he stands beside my car. His crotch is directly in front of my face, and I notice a bulge in the front of his pants. *Well... it would seem that I have the same effect on him that he does on me.* God help us both if we're ever alone together with a couple of hours on our hands. I suspect neither of us would ever be the same.

"Alright. The address of the restaurant and the time are in your calendar. Any other time I'd pick you up, but I can't tonight. I have a late afternoon appointment that I can't miss. I hope it's good for you to just meet me there."

"Yeah, fine. I prefer it, actually."

"So, you can get away if it's not going well?" He smiles, and I hope he knows I'm joking. If I'm being truthful, it's because I'm afraid of what would happen if we're alone together in a car.

"I'm sure that won't be necessary."

I glance at my phone to make sure he's really put the information in there and he's not just trying to make me look like a fool. *Why don't I trust him?* Everything looks legitimate, and he bends back down, smiling at me as he gets close to my lips again.

"See you tonight." I say.

He winks at me and says, "I'm looking forward to getting to know you." Turning around and moving toward his car, he says, "You can watch me walk away if you want."

I laugh and raise my hand to my mouth in an attempt to hide my grin. It doesn't work. Waving as he gets into his car, he drives off, leaving me sitting there grinning like an idiot.

My phone rings immediately, and I think it's him calling. *Is he canceling on me already?* Checking the screen, I remember the desperately hopeless message I left for Melea just a few minutes ago. My shoulders sink as I try to think of what to say to her now.

"Hey, hon. Sorry for the morbid message, but things have completely changed now. I'm fine, but I need your help. Forget about what I said on the voicemail. Can I video chat with you when I get home? I'll need to show you some of my clothes so you can help me pick out what to wear on my date tonight."

Chapter Seven

JOE

All the way back to work, I can't get my mind off Mary and our date tonight. I've already called the owner of the restaurant to make sure he has my favorite table ready... and that no one calls me by my real name. Given her reaction to seeing my name on the back of the cards when we first met, I'm not ready to tell her exactly who I am. Plus, I'd like to find out more of her objections to them, so I can improve the quality. If she knows I'm behind them, she may not be as honest with me as I'd like.

Am I being a hypocrite for not being completely honest with her? Probably, but I'm not trying to hurt her. I just want to get to know her without the added pressure of being someone she already has strong negative feelings about.

My relief that Mom is still at lunch when I return to the office is short-lived. There's no doubt in my mind that she's likely already heard about the incident at the bank this morning. It's one of the few banks in town, and Mom has already proved her ability to sniff out all the gossip. Especially if it involves me. And since I was at the bank this morning during the fracas, I'm certain she knows.

The frown on her face when she returns from lunch proves my hypothesis. Hoping to stop the verbal assault before it gets started, I say, "It wasn't my fault this time."

"You say that every time."

"But I mean it this time. All I was doing was having breakfast and—"

"Breakfast at the bank? How convenient they are making their services now. Do they also fill up and wash your car while you're making a deposit or cashing a check? What about checking the oil or picking up your dry cleaning?"

"Now who's being snarky?"

She inhales and exhales the way she does when I'm getting on her last nerve. "I'm your mother and am allowed. Besides, I have already received three phone calls and two text messages from women who were either in the bank during this shouting match or know someone who was. All of them said you were there, speaking with Grace at first and then a few observed you talking with the woman doing the screaming in the parking lot. Are they telling me the truth?"

"The woman doing the screaming in the parking lot, as you say, I have a date with her tonight."

"Is she the one from the store yesterday? The one with whom you are so enamored?"

I grin and nod. "I finally got her name. Mary. Isn't that the sweetest name you've ever heard?"

"You've already fallen for this young woman, haven't you?"

"I know you want me to be careful and make sure she's not after the company or anything. And I will, though I think that's the farthest thing from her mind. But, I know your concerns about having fallen for some women in the past who've not been interested in me for me. I haven't forgotten your lessons, Mother."

"Good. That's all I want to know. I want you to find someone who makes you happy, son. I just don't want you to get hurt again in the process. Please, just be careful. Guard your heart."

She looks at me as if she wants to hug me, which is a foreign concept for both of us. I don't remember the last time that happened. She's never been affectionate, but that doesn't mean she's not a doting mother. She is.

"Now, the next order of business is for us to address the copyright issue. Are you certain that Charles obtained the drawings legitimately?"

"You know, and please don't hold this over my head and bring it up in an argument later, because I'll deny ever having said it, but I think you might be right about him. You can wipe that smug look off your face, thank you very much. I know he's a jackass, Mother, but I really never thought he'd do something like this to me. I can't get him to send the paperwork, and of course, you know what trouble I had getting him to answer the phone. I'm beginning to think there's a reason he's avoiding me. Not just him being selfish and rude. But a real reason. Like maybe there's something he's trying to keep from me."

"Are you going to confront him about it?"

"Not yet. Until I have something more concrete than just a suspicion, anything I say to him now will just let him know I'm on to him. He'll try to cover his tracks even more. No, I think the best course of action is to just continue to reach out nicely, and try to get him to send the correct documents. I thought mentioning the fines would be motivation enough. If it has to do with money, he's quite cautious."

"Well, it isn't his money he stands to lose. It's yours. He feels no responsibility for safeguarding your money and your company. Having said that, I agree with your strategy. Keep your friends close and your enemies closer, as the old saying goes."

It's sad that I have to consider Charles to be an enemy, but she's right. Again. Though I won't tell her that. I still have some of my pride. "So, I was hoping we could truncate our meeting this afternoon so I could get ready for my date a little early."

"You were, were you? Well, I suppose you'd better get started on those reports on your desk if you want to be finished early. I'll send an email to the department heads asking them to submit their budget estimates now instead of waiting to present them to you at the meeting. They can explain any over-budget accounts in the email instead of discussing them with you this afternoon. That will save at least a few minutes."

"Sometimes I wonder why you gave me this company to run instead of you just managing it yourself. You're a hell of a businesswoman, Mom. And you're pretty much in charge, anyway. I'm just a figurehead."

"I've told you before, Joseph. I don't want the commitment. I want the freedom to run off to Paris whenever I want. Or go scuba diving in the Caribbean at a moment's notice. If I had to run this place, I wouldn't be able to do those things."

"When was the last time you did anything like that? To my knowledge, you've never been scuba diving in your life."

"But the point is that I *could* do it whenever. Now, if you'll excuse me, I have an email to write."

I can't suppress the smile I have on my face.

***

"Alright, everyone. Is there anything else we need to discuss regarding your departmental budgets for next year?"

No one says anything or raises their hands. Relieved that the meeting is ending a full hour earlier than I expected, I smile. "Well, thank you all very much for being here. I'll look these over in the coming days and have any revisions back to you before we close for the Christmas holiday. You have until then to submit any changes you'd like for me to consider."

Mom stands and says, "Once he approves your budget, I'll return it to you. At that point, they lock in for the entire year. No more changes unless an extraordinary situation arises. And we'll be the ones to determine what qualifies."

Most of them leave without moaning, but I notice a few good-natured eye rolls. I smile to myself, but I'm grateful Mom didn't see them.

"I know you're anxious to leave, Joe, but I think you should attempt to call Charles again before you go. I've just received an email from the Copyright Office informing me that they still cannot process the application."

"Again? I thought what Charles had last sent over would resolve the issue. That's what he promised."

"I know, dear, but it didn't. There is good news, though. They approved our request to extend the deadline. We have another week."

That still doesn't leave us with much time, but we are running out of choices. "I'll call him right now. And if it goes to voicemail, I'll call him again and again. We don't have time for his bullshit."

The first call, as I suspected, goes straight to voicemail. So does the next one. And the one after that.

"Try not to get too upset. I know you're excited about your date tonight, and I'd hate for this foolishness to ruin it for you."

"Oh shit! I just thought of something. Why didn't I think of this before? This just might work!"

"What are you blabbering on about, Joseph?"

"When I spent Thanksgiving with Charles and his family, I met his brother-in-law. Well, actually, he wasn't actually his brother-in-law. The man had been married to Charles's late sister. They were still in business together and spent time together as a family. Anyway, I sensed a lot of tension between the two of them, and a lot of disdain toward Charles from the man's new wife."

"Sounds like a smart woman."

I resist the temptation to chastise her, basically because I'd thought the same thing about the woman. "Anyway, the thought just occurred to me that if there's hostility between Charles and members of his family, perhaps one of them would be willing to help us."

"By doing what, exactly?"

"Maybe finding out why Charles is avoiding sending the documents to me."

"Do you really think one of them would tell you that? I mean, even if there is hostility within the family, that doesn't mean anyone is willing to go behind his back. It's one thing not to like someone in your family. It's quite another to plot against the man."

"I'm not asking anyone to plot against him. I just want to get to the bottom of this, and if Charles won't answer me, I don't have many alternatives." Going quickly to my computer, I look up Charles's company to find Jordan's email address. At least, I think that's what his name is. Jordan. I scroll through the contacts and find the image of the man I met on Thanksgiving. "That's him. I'll email him and then I have to go. Remember, I have a date tonight."

Chapter Eight

MARY

Though I'm so nervous I can barely keep my com-posure, I've been daydreaming about this date for hours. "I'm happy with the dress you decided on, Mary. I think you look beautiful. I'm sure that Joshua won't be able to keep his tongue in his mouth when he sees you. Or his eyes in his head. Or his—"

"Alright, that's enough," I interrupt. "I know what you're about to say. He needs to keep it in his pants, and that's taking it a little too far, don't you think?"

"I don't know, hon. With as much misery as you've been through, I don't think it's going far enough. Anyway, what I'm trying to say, though not very elegantly, is that you look beautiful. Doesn't she, Jordan?"

Melea hands her phone to her husband and his handsome dark face takes up most of the screen. It's funny the way he still struggles with technology at times. Melea pulls the phone away from his face, and he smiles widely at me. "She's right, Mary. You look amazing! I'm glad you're doing this. It's time you got out in the dating world again. There's no reason for you to wait as long as I did to find Melea. You're young, beautiful, talented, and one of the nicest people I've ever met. You deserve to be happy."

"Thanks, Jordan. You're sweet to say so."

"Let me have the phone back," Melea says in the background.

"Alright, Mary. I guess this is goodbye. Have fun tonight."

"You, too. Tell the kids I'm sorry I can't make it to their program, but that I'm very proud of them."

"He's nodding." She stops and smiles at me through the phone. "I gotta go, babe. Everyone is itching to get out of here. Thank you for including me in this time with you. Text me when you get back home."

Before I get a chance to say I will, she's already talking to the kids and soon the screen goes black. I'm grateful she was available this afternoon to help me. It's quite likely I would've backed out more than once if she hadn't been involved. There was no way she'd let me out of it, and I'm so glad about that.

I take one more look at myself in the mirror and notice a smile begins to stretch across my face. I've never thought I was beautiful, but I can't help but feel that way right now. The little blonde girl staring back at me in the mirror approves of what she sees in her future self. I hope Joshua does, too.

Chapter Nine

JOE

Thankfully, the email didn't take long, and I got home, cleaned up, and arrived at the restaurant in record time. There aren't many people here yet, but it's still early. "Mr. McCoy. It's a pleasure as always, to have you here with us tonight."

"Don't forget, Marco. I don't want to make a big deal with my companion tonight who I am. Your staff is not to address me by my name."

"Of course. I remember, and I have instructed them all to call you 'sir' only. There will be nothing to ruin your evening. Do you know when the young lady will arrive?"

"I asked her to meet me here at 8:00. I know I'm terribly early, but I wanted to make sure things were perfect for her when she arrives. But it looks like that was unnecessary.

This looks wonderful." Marco has done an excellent job setting my favorite table up just right. The flowers are fresh, and the lighting is dim, but bright enough that I can still see the menu. Marco sends several of his waiters to the table to have me select the wine. I know it's a weird thing to say when getting ready for a date, but part of me wishes Mom was here. She's an expert on wine, and while she's tried to impart some of her knowledge to me, I'm afraid I still know very little. I take a picture of each bottle to send her, asking for a little help.

Noticing an email notification, I excitedly click on it and see it's from Jordan, Charles's brother-in-law. I dial Mom's number immediately.

"I was just about to text you back on the wine choice. Why are you so impatient?"

"Forget about the wine for a moment. I need you to do something for me as soon as you can. I just heard back from Jordan. He said he'd be glad to help, though he knows very little about Charles's department. I didn't tell him specifically what I wanted to know, so he wouldn't let it slip or get offended that I asked him and go straight to Charles. I was very vague about what I wanted."

"So, what do you need me to do?"

"Are you still at the office? Never mind. That's a stupid question. Of course, you're still at the office. So, take some pictures of the cards and send them to me. I'll send them to Jordan and explain to him exactly what we need and why.

There's a big possibility this whole thing could blow up in my face, but this is the best option I think we have."

"I agree. I'll get those pictures to you in a few minutes. Will you have time to do all this before Mary arrives?"

"Oh yeah. She won't be here for a while. I got here really early."

"Do you mean to tell me that you didn't have to leave work when you did? I could've had you for a couple of hours longer?"

"Goodbye, Mom. Send those pics to me as soon as you can. I'd like to get them to him before he leaves his office."

I hang up before she has time to protest. I laugh as I imagine the frustrated expression on her face. With no time to waste, I sit down at my favorite table and compose an email to Jordan asking for his help with the copyrights.

***

I finish the email to Jordan a few minutes after Mom sends the pictures. It took longer than I expected. How was I supposed to ask what I need him to do? *Would you mind snooping through your brother-in-law's computer to find some licensing for artwork that he's refused to send to me?* Yeah, that doesn't seem like an easy ask. I had to phrase it just right.

Sending it before Mary arrives was my main priority. I'd hope to catch him at his office, but if I have to wait until tomorrow, that's fine. I'd rather spend the next few hours thinking about Mary and nothing else. They're calling for snow tonight, so I thought it would be fun to take her for a carriage ride through town. Luckily, when you live in a small farming town, there's always someone with a carriage and some horses. I wonder if I should plan for one to pick us up shortly after dinner. I text a carriage owner I know, and he replies he'll be ready if I want. All I have to do is let him know.

Now all that's left to do is wait for her to arrive. I've checked my watch probably fifty times, along with keeping an eye on the clock on my phone when I was writing the email to Jordan. My stomach is doing flips the closer it gets to 8:00, but I do everything I can to stay calm. I check my phone every time I get a notification, thinking it could be Mom or Jordan, but fearing it could also be Mary canceling on me.

I don't have to wait much longer. Marco opens the door to the private dining room and escorts the gorgeous creature to my table. I stand as she arrives, but my mouth is dry, and I don't have any words.

She smiles timidly and says, "Hi."

A waiter suddenly appears to hold her chair as Marco guides her into it. Kissing her hand and bowing to me, he leaves, and I settle back into my own chair. "Hi, yourself.

You look amazing." She blushes, and it's the cutest thing I think I've ever seen. Immediately my mind takes me to a vision of her underneath me, face flushing with pleasure, not embarrassment. Before I embarrass her further by throwing her across the table and taking her right here, I turn to the waiter and order wine. He nods and speeds off toward the kitchen.

"You look amazing, too," she says. "I haven't lived here long and don't get out much, but I didn't know this place was here. There can't be many elegant restaurants like this around. Do you come here often?"

I do, but I can't tell her that. I entertain business clients here frequently, and this is where Mom and I usually have celebratory dinners. Mary can't know that. I don't want her to catch on to who I really am, or she might leave. "I've been here a couple of times, but yes, this is the only restaurant of this caliber in town."

"Well, it's lovely. I haven't been to a nice place like this in a long time. Thank you for inviting me."

"Someone should take you to nice places all the time. Someone like you should never have to settle for anything less."

She narrows her eyes at me. "Now, how would you know? You don't know anything about me."

"I don't have to know. All I have to do is look at you and I think you deserve nothing but the best in life. This is going to sound presumptuous, but I'm going to say it, anyway. I want to show you everything beautiful in the world. You make me want to find the beauty in the smallest things, and I've never had anyone make me feel the way you do. I don't know exactly what's going on between us, but I think it could be something special."

She swallows hard and takes a sip of water. *Shit! I've said too much and scared her away.*

"I feel the same way about you, Joshua. You've been on my mind since we met in the store. My father would say I'm being foolish and to take things slowly, but I don't want to. And I just can't get you out of my head."

"I like that song, and the sentiment," I grin. "I guess we're a couple of fools rushing in. I don't know if that's a movie or a song. I hope it's a song."

"Do you always compare emotions to songs?"

I chuckle. "Yes, I suppose I do, though no one has ever really called me on it like this."

The rest of the evening is magical. Whenever our eyes meet, or we both reach for the bread at the same time and our hands touch, I'm forced to resist every urge I have. Nasty urges. Filthy urges. Beautiful urges. If I'm reading the expression on her face correctly, she's fighting those same urges.

After dinner, I suggest the carriage ride as we leave the restaurant. "Really? There's something like that in this town?"

"Oh, yeah, honey. We don't have many tourists come through here, but we have a few, especially at Christmas. It's one of the things we're famous for."

"One of them? There are other things you're famous for?"

"You're just going to have to stick with me and find out."

"I think I can do that," she says and both my heart and my cock swell. When I open the door, she gasps. "Oh look! It's snowing!"

"So, is that a yes on the carriage ride?"

Her eyes fall to the ground, and I think she's about to break my heart despite all the wonderful things she's said tonight about her feelings toward me. When she lifts her head, I see something unmistakable in her eyes. Something I've felt since the moment I saw her. Something that makes every nerve ending in my body come alive.

Desire.

"Actually, I was wondering if you'd like to come back to my place. It's not much, but I have a fireplace, some wine, and a great view of the most beautiful tree-lined field you've ever seen in your life. I imagine it will be even more spectacular covered with snow."

"Mary, I really want to kiss you right now. Would that be alright with you?"

"I'd be terribly disappointed if you didn't."

My arms wrap around her waist, almost as if they have minds of their own. I pull her close to me, her scent intoxicating me. "You smell like what I imagine heaven must smell like." Her lips curl into a smile, but I don't give her an opportunity to say a word as mine gently brushes against hers.

The kiss is soft and timid at first, and suddenly I'm overcome with passion. My tongue darts forward, parting her lips, and plunging into her welcoming mouth. She places her hands on my face, and despite the cold, her fingers are hot as they explore my face just as I explore her mouth.

It's only when I hear a man behind me clearing his throat that I realize there's another person in the world besides the two of us at this moment. She pulls away from me and her eyes in a shy grin as we move a little to the left, allowing the couple to enter the restaurant. "We should probably get out of here before someone calls the cops on us."

Chapter Ten

MARY

With Joshua standing so close behind me, I have a hard time getting the door unlocked. We laugh when I drop the keys for the second time. "I can't concentrate on anything but you," I tell him.

"Yeah, I know the feeling. Give me the keys and let me try. If one of us doesn't get this door open soon, we'll have two frostbitten asses in the morning, because I want you right now. And I'm going to start peeling off clothes in just a few seconds."

"Good thing I don't have any neighbors on this side of the house. Now if we were in the front, we'd give the whole street a show."

Since the prospect of frostbite on my ass doesn't appeal to me, I'm thankful he gets the door open quickly. My pussy is especially thankful.

We're barely in the door before we both begin removing clothes. I turn my back to him and point to the zipper at the base of my neck. Time slows as he lowers it all the way to the base of my spine, allowing the slinky dress to fall to the floor. A guttural sound emanates from the back of his throat when he realizes I'm not wearing a bra, and my little black lace panties, drenched by my desire, fall on top of my dress.

"Want to know a secret?" I ask as I step out of my clothes and slowly turn around to face him. He nods, and his rapt expression makes me wonder if he is capable of speaking now. "I wouldn't have cared about frostbite, or neighbors, or pesky things like clothes. I would have let you peel them off of me, because there's nothing more that I want right now than for you to fuck me."

His mouth crashes into mine, and I press my body into his. I gasp as something hard presses into my belly. He didn't have time to remove his underwear before I completely distracted him with my zipper, but that doesn't prevent me from feeling every inch of his thick cock on my skin. Aching for it to be inside me, I grip the waistband of his boxers and slowly lower them to the floor. With his glorious cock standing erect in front of my face, I lean forward, preparing to take him into my mouth.

He grabs me by the waist and pulls me to my feet. "Oh, no, baby. There's no time for that." He spins me around and gently bends me over the back of the couch. With his hands on my hips, he lifts my ass into the air. "I have to be inside you right now or I'll die!"

And in a moment, he is. We both gasp as he enters me from behind. He lingers inside me for a moment, allowing my pussy to conform to him before pulling all the way out and thrusting in again. My entire body tingles, and if I didn't know any better, I'd think he's fucking me with a lightning rod. Every motion creates another incredible sensation in my core. "Oh, God! You feel so fucking good inside me. Don't stop. Please don't ever stop."

"Not on your life, baby. I'm not stopping until we're both spent."

And he doesn't. Each thrust, every moan, every touch brings me closer to the precipice, and I'm not able to stop the crashing waves inside my body. "I'm coming!" I scream, as if he doesn't already know that.

He says nothing intelligible, and neither do I until our bodies explode in release. Holding himself in me until I stop convulsing, he pulls out and collapses on top of me, stretching himself across my back. His hands never stop caressing my sides, my arms, my ass, and anything else he can touch.

"Where's your bedroom?" he whispers into my ear. I'm unable to speak, so I just point down the hallway. He sweeps down to pick me up and carries me into my bedroom, my head nestled against his shoulder. Gently placing me on the bed, he climbs in beside me. We hold each other until sleep claims us.

***

The sun creeping in the window is warm against my skin, despite the chill in the air. Joshua's arms fold around me and squeeze, making me feel safe. It's been a long time since I've felt that way in a man's arms. And it feels so good.

"Good morning," he says, startling me. "I wasn't sure if you were awake, and you felt so good lying beside me. I didn't want to disturb you."

"So last night wasn't a dream, was it?"

He chuckles. "No baby, it wasn't. And even if it was, it was the best fucking dream I've ever had in my life."

"Are you hungry? I'm not much of a cook, but I think I have some eggs in the fridge, and I can definitely make coffee."

"Well, I *can* cook, so show me the way to the kitchen and allow me to make breakfast for you. You can make the coffee."

We smile shyly at each other as we gather our clothes from the living room floor. I had the luxury of having pajamas to put on, and I dug around in the closet for something that he might be able to wear. As much as I would rather not see him in it, the only thing I have is an old bathrobe that belonged to Charles. I'm surprised I have it, but I try to put that, and him, out of my mind.

"What's this?" he asks and points to my drawing table in the corner of the living room.

"Oh, I suppose we were a little preoccupied when we came in last night, and I didn't give you the grand tour. That's where I work."

"You're an artist?"

"Yeah, I am. Art has always been a passion of mine. When I started over after the divorce, I decided to make it my career." I put my hand on his shoulder as I come up behind him so I can show him some of my designs. "Lately I've been working on these, but these are what I already have for sale in my shop."

A strange look crosses his face, and I wonder if he's beginning to have regrets about last night. I try to put that thought out of my head. "You know, I probably need to send a text to my assistant instructing her not to come in today. Wouldn't want her barging in on us." I smile, but he looks at me as if he is getting sick. *Yep. He's definitely having second thoughts.* I grab my phone and quickly text Paulina. I see an urgent message from Melea, and I click over to it.

Just as I'm about to ask Joshua if he's feeling alright or if he needs to sit down, the message from Melea appears on the screen. As my eyes fall over the words she's written, my blood begins to boil. "Oh, my God! This is a text from my best friend. She said a friend of my ex-husband's contacted her husband yesterday regarding some of my designs. Something weird is happening. She said he forwarded the guy's email to me."

Joshua turns away and slowly walks to the couch. A rush of excitement comes over me, and I have to suppress a grin as the memory of what we did on that couch last night enters my head. He sits, and I notice that the look of illness on his face has become one of panic. Not sure what to do to help him, I return my attention to my phone as the email appears.

"Don't read that email, please."

He says it too late. I've already read it. As I scroll through to the bottom, I see recognize the company logo. If I'm not mistaken, it's the same one that was on the back of the cards I saw at the store. The day I first met Joshua. I remember that Paulina had brought a package of them to show me. I rush to my drafting table and find them and compare. I'm right. It's the same logo.

"What? Someone is stealing my designs? I can't believe this! Who the hell would do something like this?"

I notice an image loading at the bottom of the email, just underneath the logo. "There's a name. Joe McCoy. The name of the bastard who's conspiring with my ex-husband to steal my designs is Joe McCoy! He apparently

went to school with Charles and they recently reconnect-
ed. Charles sent some of my designs that I didn't even
know he had to this guy and he's selling those cards with
inferior copies of mine. You remember, don't you, Joshua?
They're the ones we talked about in the store the first day
we met. Oh, good... there's a picture of this Joe McCoy
under the signature on the email. It's just taking a minute
to load. Wait until I get my hands on those two! I'll sue
them both for everything they have!"

The image finally loads of Joe McCoy, and it guts me.
I look up at Joshua, who's still sitting on the couch. He
doesn't look sick or panicked any longer, but he has tears
in his eyes. Now I'm the one who might throw up.

Quietly, he says, "I can explain."

Chapter Eleven

JOE

Mom stands in front of me wearing a dubious expression. "Are you sure you want to do this, son? This has the potential to really blow up in your face."

"I don't have much of a choice, Mom. I love her, and nothing will be right with me until I make this up to her."

"But she still hasn't agreed to see you, despite Charles explaining everything to her. Telling her that he was the one who stole her designs and deceived you when he sold them to you. You've pulled all the cards off the shelves and withdrawn the copyright applications. It hasn't seemed to matter. She's still furious with you. With you both. Even her friend Melea tried to convince her you're innocent of all this."

"I know all this, Mom, but once again, this is the only thing I know to do. The one thing I'm not innocent of is lying to her. I told her the wrong name, and I slept with her when she thought I was someone else. My only hope is that she'll get caught up in the Christmas spirit and be able to find it in herself to forgive me."

Mom shakes her head, but smiles at me anyway. "Alright. Let's get this show on the road, then. It's cold out here." She slips the elastic around the back of my neck and chuckles as she adjusts the fake white beard on my chin. "You look ridiculous, by the way. But you're also one of the kindest people I've ever known. So, if anyone can play Santa and be convincing, it's you."

"Thanks, Mom."

"Just a little secret I want to share with you. I've accomplished a lot of things in my life, and I've seen even more. I'd always thought the proudest moment in my life was when I gave birth to you. But I've changed my mind. I'm most proud of you today. I know I don't say it enough, but I love you."

Words escape me, and all I can do is hug her.

***

Christmas music blasts through the loudspeaker as I walk into the community center. The pastor of the church told me to expect about thirty children, but I think there are twice that. At least.

"And here he is, kids. The one… The only Santa Claus!!! Let's hear a round of applause." Kids scream and cheer while their parents look around with a mixture of joy and wonder on their tear-stained faces.

Though I smile at all the children as they jump up and down clamoring for the gifts I've brought for them, my head spins around, looking for Mary. She's supposed to be here, at least that's what Melea told me, but I don't see her. Maybe she was too upset to volunteer, though her friends told me she always spends Christmas Eve passing out gifts to children who otherwise wouldn't have any. I understand she was actually looking forward to it this year, since the last couple of weeks have been so hard on her.

As I pass out the last gift in my bag, my hand brushes up against the one in my pocket. The one it looks as if I'll not be able to give.

I look at Mom standing in the corner and notice her pointing behind me. I spin around and see my beautiful angel looking around at all the smiling little faces. She's smiling, too. I'm relieved. I wondered if I'd ever see her smile again.

Taking a deep breath to steady my nerves, I tell myself it's show time and make my way through the crowd of children and parents to her.

"Well, hello, Santa. We had such a wonderful turnout today. Thank you for doing this. I know it means so much to the kids and their families."

"Mary, please don't be angry. It's me. Joe."

She stiffens and I begin to lose my resolve. "What are you doing here? I think I've made it clear that I don't want to see you."

"Yes, you have, but honey, I just can't accept that. I wanted to see you one more time and tell you how sorry I am. If you hear me out right now and still feel the same way, I'll leave you alone. I promise."

"Fine."

"Thank you. I had nothing to do with stealing your designs. I told you. Charles told you. And Melea and Jordon both told you they believed me. I understand that you believe me, and that you don't hold it against me. What you're angry about is that I lied to you. Well, honey, you're right. I screwed up. I lied to you, and I am so sorry. Nothing I can say will change that. Even if you believe me when I say I only lied because I was afraid. Afraid of losing you before we had a chance to see if we could fall in love. Then, I did fall in love with you, and I planned to tell you the truth. I just didn't know how. But you have to believe that I loved you then, and I love you now."

Tears fill her eyes. "What are you talking about, Joe? You love me? Where I come from, people don't lie to someone they love. I want to believe you, but I've been burned before, and all I want is to trust the man I love. I want to trust you."

"I know. And that's why I'm begging you to forgive me." I stop as I realize what she just said. "Wait. Are you saying that you love me, too?"

She glances around the room and blushes. Everyone else is quiet and paying attention only to us... well, except for the youngest children.

"Joe, does your mother have a camera pointed at us?"

"Yes, she's on video chat right now with Melea. Do you see that everyone is interested in your answer? It's Christmas, honey. Please forgive me and say you love me."

She breaks into a smile and says, "Well, I'd hate to disappoint all these people. Yes, I love you, and I forgive you. Actually, I forgave you as soon as Charles explained everything to me. I was just still so hurt. I wanted some time to process my emotions. I've been so miserable without you. But if I take you back, you must promise me you'll never lie to me again."

"I promise." I reach into my pocket and pull out the last gift I haven't passed out yet. "I'm not going to get on one knee here in front of all these kids. They might get confused to see Santa propose to you, but I'm quietly going to ask you, anyway." I lean in to her ear and say, "Please... marry me, Mary."

She nods as tears roll down her face.

A little girl sitting in front of us giggles and points above our heads. "You have to kiss her, Santa. You're standing underneath the mistletoe."

I grin and we both look up. "Indeed, we are," I laugh. "How do you like that?"

"I like it very much," Mary says, and gently pulls me to her for a kiss. The room erupts into cheers, and she giggles. "Your beard is scratchy."

<h1 style="text-align:center">Epilogue</h1>

<h2 style="text-align:center">JOE</h2>

One Year Later

Mary and Mom stand off to the side, smirking at me as I look in the mirror.

"Until one of you two ladies wants to put on this Santa suit, I don't think there's anything for you to laugh at."

"Though Santa is supposed to have a big belly, I don't think he's supposed to be as big as a house."

Melea laughs from the other side of the room. "I'd worry that a pregnant Santa might traumatize the kids for the rest of their lives."

"Is that why you refused to dress like an elf, darling?" Jordan asks as he puts his arms around her. "You thought it would be too much for them to see a pregnant Santa and a pregnant elf?"

"Something like that," she says and elbows him gently in the side. "Though I mostly didn't think I could squeeze into that thing. Charles? What do you think? Would I fit in there with my big pregnant belly?"

We all laugh as Charles comes into the room dressed as the biggest elf in the world. "You can make fun of me all you want, but I'm going to enjoy this."

The pastor sticks his head in the door and says, "Alright Santa and very large Elf. I think the kids are ready for you."

"Show time," I say.

Everyone files out of the room except for Mary, who walks over to Charles and me. She takes his hand and says, "I'm glad I don't hate you anymore. Life is too short for that. Thank you for all you've done to support my business this year and thank you for donating all these toys. The kids are going to love it."

"Well, I figured I've done enough bad things in my life. I'd better start trying to balance that out before it's too late. Thank *you* for allowing me to be your friend." He looks at me and says, "Both of you."

He walks away, but stops before he gets out the door. "Hey, Joe? I saw Grace Herndon from the bank out there. I think we hit it off when we met earlier. That alright with you?"

"I wouldn't have said this a year ago, but, yeah, man, it's fine with me. Gracie is a wonderful woman, a good friend of mine, and she deserves to be happy. So do you."

When he leaves, Mary pulls me down to kiss her. "If I didn't know any better," she says, "I'd think there was a tear in his eye. What do you think?"

"I think I'm the luckiest man on the face of the planet." I kiss her again. This time, it's more than just a peck on the lips.

She ends the kiss and says, "That was probably not appropriate behavior for a church on Christmas Eve."

"Nonsense. You know we were always supposed to be together, don't you? Especially on Christmas?"

"What *are* you talking about now, Santa, dear? Have you already had too much eggnog?"

I take her hand as we walk to the door, hearing the Christmas music playing over the loudspeaker. "I mean, really. Think about it. Our names are Mary and Joseph. You're pregnant, and you gave me the greatest gifts I could ever have.... You and our baby! What could be more Christmas-y than that?"

***

Keep reading to see all the books in ***A Country Christmas***

***

Want to be among the first to know everything about my books? Join my newsletter... also get a freebie! https://www.subscribepage.com/j9h4o1

More Books by Bree Weeks

Feels Like the First Time
I Want You to Want Me
Some Kind of Wonderful
Somebody to Love
Dream On
Take It To the Limit

Thankful Hearts (4-book series)
The Trouble With Hello
Love Out of Time
An Inconvenient Flame
Role of the Heart

*United For Love (Series Starters - Loving His Workout, Feels Like the First Time, and The Trouble With Hello)

Mending Broken Hearts (3-book series)

Splintered Hearts
Slivered Hearts
Shattered Hearts

<u>Not the Good Guy Series - with Kyra Nyx (3-book series)</u>
<u>Of Wicked Things</u>
<u>Of Broken Things</u>
<u>Of Lost Things</u>

Collaborations and Stand Alones
<u>Cracks in the Windshield</u> - part of the After I Do series
<u>Beginner's Luck</u> - part of the Get Lucky series
<u>Love Half-Baked</u> - part of the In Praise of Older Women series
<u>Sweet Child O' Mine</u> - part of the 80s Baby 2 series
<u>The Widower Takes a Wife</u> - part of the May December Romance series
<u>Summer Savory</u> - part of the Mountain Ridge Resort series
<u>Love's Faithful Vow</u> - part of the Endless Obsession series
<u>Juke Move</u> - part of the Gridiron Love series
<u>Slick</u> - part of the Dirty Sinners series
<u>The Taste of Kindness</u> - part of the Vices & Virtues series
<u>Mary Didn't Know</u> – part of A Country Christmas series
<u>Naughty and Nice</u> – part of the Christmas Falls series

About the Author and Connect with Bree

Bree Weeks writes steamy short reads that may just make you blush. She believes in love at first sight, the power of a good story, and that college football and a good HEA are the greatest things ever.

She lives just south of Nashville, Tennessee, with her husband and their dogs. When she's not writing, she loves to connect with her fans, cook good old-fashioned southern food, and spending time with her grandchildren.

Connect With Bree

Facebook: https://www.facebook.com/BreeWeeksAuthor/

Instagram: https://www.instagram.com/breeweeksauth
or/
Twitter: https://twitter.com/bree_author
Website: https://www.breeweeksauthor.com/